Franklin and His Friend

From an episode of the animated TV series *Franklin* produced by
Nelvana Limited, Neurones France s.a.r.l. and Neurones Luxembourg S.A.

Based on the Franklin books by Paulette Bourgeois and Brenda Clark.
TV tie-in adaptation written by Sharon Jennings and illustrated by
Mark Koren, Alice Sinkner, and Jelena Sisic.
TV episode written by Ken Ross.

Franklin is a trade mark of Kids Can Press Ltd.

Kids Can Press is a *Corus*™ Entertainment company

The character Franklin was created by Paulette Bourgeois and Brenda Clark.

No part of this publication may be reproduced in whole or in part, or stored
in a retrieval system, or transmitted in any form or by any means, electronic,
mechanical, photocopying, recording, or otherwise, without written
permission of the publisher. For information regarding permission, write to
Kids Can Press Ltd., 29 Birch Avenue, Toronto, Ontario, Canada M4V 1E2.

ISBN 0-439-33878-6

Text copyright © 2002 by Contextx Inc.
Illustrations copyright © 2002 by Brenda Clark Illustrator Inc.

All rights reserved. Published by Scholastic Inc., 557 Broadway, New York, NY
10012, by arrangement with Kids Can Press Ltd. SCHOLASTIC and associated
logos are trademarks and/or registered trademarks of Scholastic Inc.

12 11 10 9 8 7 6 5 4 3 2 1   1 2 3 4 5 6/0

Printed in the U.S.A.   23

First Scholastic printing, August 2002

Franklin and His Friend

SCHOLASTIC INC.

New York   Toronto   London   Auckland   Sydney
Mexico City   New Delhi   Hong Kong   Buenos Aires

KINGSWAY
CHRISTIAN
SCHOOL
LIBRARY

FRANKLIN had lots of good friends and a best friend named Bear. He also had a friend named Otter, who had moved away. Franklin and Otter sent each other birthday cards and photographs, but they hadn't seen each other for a long time. Then, one day, a very special letter arrived for Franklin. Otter was coming to visit.

Franklin hurried to Bear's house with his news.

"Guess what?!" he exclaimed. "Otter's coming to stay with her grandma this weekend!"

"Hooray!" said Bear.

"Remember the old days when we used to slip and slide down the riverbank?" Franklin asked.

"Gee, Franklin," replied Bear. "Nobody does *that* anymore."

"Well, I bet Otter will want to," said Franklin.

On his way home, Franklin stopped by the pond. He told Beaver about Otter's visit.

"Remember all the swimming races we used to have?" Franklin asked. "I bet Otter can't wait to race us again."

"Otter is captain of a swim team now," replied Beaver. "She won't want to race us slowpokes."

"Yes, she will," Franklin insisted.

Beaver rolled her eyes.

When he got home, Franklin went to his room. He searched and searched through his toy box, under his dresser, and in his closet. Then he called his mother.

"Where are my blocks?" he asked.

"You gave them to Harriet," she answered. "You said you didn't need them anymore."

"Well, now I want them back," said Franklin. "Otter and I always played with those blocks."

He marched off to Harriet's bedroom.

Finally, the big day arrived. Otter was coming for lunch.

Franklin sat on the front steps all morning.

"When is she going to get here?" he said over and over. "I can't wait."

And suddenly, there was Otter, walking through the gate.

Franklin and his family gave Otter a big hug and a big welcome. His parents asked her lots of questions about her new home.

Franklin got out the food. "We made happy-face sandwiches just for you," he said.

"I thought those were for Harriet," said Otter.

"They're your favorite," Franklin reminded her.

Otter laughed. "That was *ages* ago."

She took a sandwich from the grown-up plate.

Franklin frowned.

After lunch, Franklin suggested they play with his blocks.

"Remember all the castles we used to build?" he asked.

Otter nodded and followed Franklin to his bedroom. Harriet was already there. She had all the blocks in her lap.

"Mine!" she said.

"I guess blocks are for babies," said Otter.

"I guess," Franklin mumbled.

Franklin and Otter went outside to play.
"Do you still go to the pond?" asked Otter.
"Of course I do," said Franklin. "Let's go!
Everyone will be there."

Franklin was right. They got to the pond, and
the whole gang was excited to see Otter. Beaver
wanted to know how many swimming medals Otter
had won. Franklin suggested they have a race.

"Oh, Franklin," said Beaver. "Otter's too good
a swimmer for us now."

But Franklin was already in the pond.
Otter jumped in beside him.
"Ready. Set. Go!" cried Bear.
Otter was across the pond before Franklin had
swum three strokes.
"Told you so," said Beaver.
Everybody laughed, even Franklin.

Franklin climbed out of the pond.

"Let's play baseball," he suggested.

"I haven't played baseball since I moved," said Otter. "I won't be any good."

Sure enough, Otter struck out on all her turns at bat, and she didn't catch a single ball heading her way.

"I don't want to play anymore," said Otter.

Franklin looked at Otter and sighed.

Just then, Otter's grandma came to get her.

"Will you play with me tomorrow, Franklin?" Otter asked.

"I guess so," replied Franklin.

Otter left, and Franklin walked home alone.

"Hmmphf!" he muttered. "We sure didn't play much today."

Franklin stomped into his house.

"Otter's no fun anymore," he announced. He told his mother about his afternoon.

His mother gave him a hug.

"You've both grown up a bit," she told him. "You've both changed."

"Does that mean we can't be friends anymore?" Franklin asked.

"Maybe," replied his mother. "Or maybe you can find a new way to stay friends."

"Hmmm," said Franklin.

The next morning, Franklin called on Otter bright and early.

"If you still lived in Woodland," Franklin told her, "you'd be a really good baseball player by now."

Then he added, "I'm going to teach you, so every time you visit, you can play on my team."

"Okay," agreed Otter. "And I'm going to teach you to be a faster swimmer. That way, every time I visit, you can race me."

The two friends smiled at each other.

Franklin and Otter spent the day racing in the pond and hitting balls out of the park.

"Today was fun," said Franklin.

"And it was fun yesterday remembering all the things we used to do together," Otter said.

"It was?" asked Franklin.

Otter nodded.

"But I remember something I guess you've forgotten," she said.

Otter grabbed Franklin's hand and pulled him up to the top of the hill. And together, the two friends went slipping and sliding down the riverbank and into the water.

Franklin laughed.

It was just like the old days.